The Big One

A Prepper series Romance

By
Louisa Bacio

Copyright © 2016 by Louisa Bacio
ISBN: 978-1-61333-978-7
Cover art by Tibbs Designs

Published by Decadent Publishing Company, LLC
Look for us online at:
www.decadentpublishing.com

Praise for *The Big One*

**2nd place Book Buyers Best, OCC/RWA
5th Place Passionate Plume, Passionate
Ink RWA
Finalist, Bookie, Best Novella**

*The romance between the two is very believable.
Sebastian was a great mix of hot male yet a bit
vulnerable.* ~ Vanessa, Amazon Reviewer

*I could not put this story down. Kayla and
Sebastian's characters are fascinating and their
love story was beautiful to watch unfold.* ~
Susan J, Amazon Reviewer

I loved this story and highly recommend it! ~ Russann Keller, Amazon Reviewer

Louisa has a way of weaving intimacy which allows me to get lost in the story. I love that!!! ~ Louisa has a way of weaving intimacy which allows me to get lost in the story. I love that!!! ~ Heather S., Amazon Reviewer

Two opposites attracting, danger, sexual escapades ~ Lisa, Pen-the-dream.blogspot.com

It's one hot, satisfying erotic short novella, taking a musician and a survivalist to a whole new level of relationship.~ Kay Dee Royal, Amazon Reviewer

The chemistry they shared left you wanting more! ~ Scotty, Amazon Reviewer

~A Note from the Author~

This story was started on December 12, 2012 (yes, 12/12/12), and the college where I teach under "lockdown" with armed suspects somewhere on campus. Nine hours of being held in the library – the same library where a campus custodian killed seven people, and injured two in 1976.

While I tried not to think of those elements too much, the experience of being "sheltered in place" inspired this tale.

Remember, be prepared!

Louisa

Chapter One

"Can you do me a favor?"

Kayla pulled the phone from her ear to glance at the screen. While caller ID indicated it was her workmate calling her early on a Friday morning, the voice coming over the phone clearly belonged to her boss, Josh.

"Um, sure. What do you need?" She hadn't left for the office yet, and she winced at his potential request. His "do me a favor" often meant stopping at the dry cleaner or dropping his dog, Cujo the Pomeranian, at the groomers. On Fridays, she liked to get into work early and back home for the weekend.

"We've got this new client, the UK Underground, and they're looking for a cool place to shoot their next video. Rumor has it you might have a bunker."

She flushed. Few people at work knew about the

hideaway, which narrowed down the field of who could have blabbed.

"It's not much," she backtracked. "Some supplies I've tucked away, just in case—r"

"I don't care why. Do you, or don't you, have a basement hidey-hole?"

"I do."

"Great. The lead singer, Sebastian, will be over at your place around noon, which gives you enough time to spruce it up a bit, you know, make it look saleable."

When Josh got excited about a project, he rambled. The last thing she wanted to do was entertain a rock star. She'd heard the excited grumblings about the new band, but didn't follow popular music too much. She saw celebrities in an "other" category, not really part of her social circles. Could she get out of it?

"Um, is it necessary?"

The line grew quiet, and then, finally, Josh cleared his throat. "Is it necessary to keep one of our newest, biggest clients happy, especially in this down economy? Oh, yes it is. And if, for some reason, we lose this account, the company may just have to undergo layoffs. Do you understand me?"

"Yes, sir." Kayla resigned herself to doing whatever was best for the company, no matter how much she'd rather not.

"So, yeah, go make yourself presentable." She heard rustling in the background and someone's muted voice.

Jacqueline? She knew the call had come from her co-worker and best friend's cell phone. So they were sleeping together? A little TMI this early in the morning.

"And Jackie says to wear your yellow sundress. It looks good on you."

With that parting comment, he hung up.

Kayla stared at the now-silent phone. What would it feel like to toss it against the wall? Resisting, she sighed and placed it on the counter. As an assistant creative director for a marketing firm, she rarely interacted with clients. Usually the message was passed down from the higher-ups. First thing she was going to do was turn on her curling iron and, while it was heating up, she was going to check out who this Sebastian from the UK Underground was anyway.

***

3

About two-thirty, she saw from her kitchen window her noon "date" coming up the walkway, looking like he'd rolled out of bed and slung on last night's clothes. How could jeans get so wrinkled? Then again, her dad, who was a retired Marine, used to press his Levi's, so she wasn't used to such sloppiness. His black leather jacket molded to his body, stretched across his shoulders, and tapered toward his waist without even being zipped.

From what she'd read in the online gossip, Sebastian was known as a heavy partier who liked to frequent Hollywood clubs. In more recent months, though, there'd been fewer sightings. Some rumors even mentioned potential problems within the band, and "creative inspiration."

Kayla knew better than to believe everything she read on the Internet, but he still lived in a much different world than she did. Seeing him, though, made her immediately think "star." Uneasiness fluttered in her stomach.

He rang her doorbell, a long, squeaking push of the button droning on as she approached.

"All right, already. I'm coming. I get it. You're here." *For crying out loud, have a little bit of*

4

patience, especially for being several hours late.

She opened the door and looked up into gray eyes. The right side of his mouth curled up, and her pulse did a corresponding jump. His magnetic star quality reached out and grabbed her by the libido. Her heart beat so fast, she felt like it was about to bust her chest. Looking at him reminded her of flipping through teen heartthrob mags—the bad-boy rocker from her teenage fantasies now stood in front of her.

She shook off the daydream. She wasn't a teen anymore, but a professional.

"Bloody hell, I had to trek all the way out here, the least you could do is open the door for me."

He walked right by her, checking out her home. Kayla stepped back, a bit unsure at his greeting.

"Umm, excuse me, and you are?" She knew damn well who he was, but she wouldn't give him the satisfaction.

"How many blokes you expecting this afternoon?" He turned, and she drew in her breath at the sight of him. The pictures online didn't do him justice. In the flesh.... She wanted to touch him. "I'm Sebastian Cox, but I figured you already knew that considering we had an appointment."

5

Anger and embarrassment replaced the instant attraction, causing the hairs on the back of her neck to stand up. He was the musician, the rock star, and she was the lowly advertising assistant. She gritted her teeth. Her company needed him, not the other way around. She had to be polite.

"Well come on in, make yourself comfortable...."

Thank God, he missed her sarcasm. She didn't entertain clients, lacked the finesse, and preferred to hide behind flow charts and spreadsheets.

He carried a red guitar case slung over the back of his shoulder. Not sure how she hadn't noticed. Must have been his bubbly personality.

"Well, where's this bunker of yours?" he said. "Let's go check out the acoustics of the bad boy."

If he wanted to be all business and get the hell out of there fast, it was fine by her. She led him through the house and out the side door. When she got to the bunker, she blocked his view of the fingerprint-and-combo lock on the outside with her body. No need for him to see the code.

The door opened without a squeak. She made sure to keep it in good condition, which included plenty of lubrication and changing the batteries when daylight savings clicked over. No one would want rusty hinges or a dead cell impeding an escape route.

She walked inside and flicked on the lights, which cast a muted glow as they charged up.

"Bloody dark down here," he commented to no one in particular as he followed her inside. "If we did the shoot here, we'd have to bring in a hell of a lot of lights." He plopped down on one of the cots, and the open V-neck of his white button-up shirt gaped further, exposing a tanned chest with a sparse covering of hair.

She looked away. He might be a smart ass, but he sure was pretty to look at. His short dark hair spiked every which way, but appeared soft to touch. She bet his stubble stayed the perfect length at all times. Maybe having him around for a few days wouldn't be so bad after all. A little bit of eye candy wouldn't do her any harm. Her friends kept telling her she needed to lighten up and stop worrying about all of the what-ifs. Well, maybe this would be her chance. Despite working in marketing, it wasn't like she interacted with star clients—ever—and if the world wanted to shake things up by laying a male specimen like Sebastian literally on her doorstep, she shouldn't waste the opportunity.

The bird from the advertising firm was wound up tighter than a farmer facing a drought. Sebastian'd had no idea what to expect when the agent called and suggested he come look at this location. An advertising agency assistant with an emergency bunker? Sure, they had them back home, littered all over England as remnants from the Cold War, but he'd imagined some old biddy owning one, walking with a cane, and smelling of lavender.

What had he ended up with? She reminded him of a sexy schoolteacher who acted like she had no idea of her own beauty. That alone could be quite appealing, if he didn't keep thinking, "freak." Despite the perfectness of this location, maybe he should consider changing the mock-up for the video. He'd been hoping for a change of pace to rock him out of his stalled writing. Trapped within his high-pressure world, nothing inspired him.

Diving headfirst into his fears might not be the answer. Being underground was already giving him the creeps. He couldn't wait to get the hell out of there. He didn't consider his case of claustrophobia all that bad, but every now and then it hit hard. The unfriendly nature of the assistant—no need to learn her name as he wasn't going to see her again—added to the discomfort.

"Hey listen," he said. "I don't think—"

A low grumble rose from the earth, one that seemed to come from all around. The ground lurched upward, throwing them to the side. Someone screamed. Oh God, it was him screaming, and he clutched at name-name-name?

"Stay calm," Kayla said. He grabbed onto her—tight—and she patted his hand while she attempted to stay upright. "Feels like a little earthquake. We're safe; let's just ride it out."

A gigantic moan emerged from the depths of the earth. All movement stopped for a beat, and then the ground surged, tossing them right and then left.

He shut his eyes, nausea tumbling through his stomach.

A beeping began. He reached out to grab hold of something to steady himself, but found nothing. His knees shook as much as the earth, and his stomach lurched up in his throat. He tasted his own fear. It couldn't be happening again. No fucking way.

The earth protested like it was going to open up and swallow him whole—swallow him alive—and then he'd suffocate, trapped under the weight of the world. He opened his mouth to ask her what the hell was going on, but before he could, she stumbled into him, hand clutched at the back of her head. A large can, which must had been on a shelf behind her, clattered to the ground. He watched her fall, but he couldn't save her—or himself.

He willed himself to move forward to check on her, and was almost convinced, when a second beeping sounded. The sick scrape of metal sliding into metal grated against his ears with a definitive locking noise.

We're fucked, he thought, and then the lights blinked off.

Chapter Two

Kayla woke in a haze, unsure of her surroundings. She could hear singing, a soft, sensual sound, and a cushion supported her head while a faint light illuminated the room. She attempted to sit up, and the bed spun. Holding onto her head, she fell backward with a moan.

She started when a figured leaned forward from the shadows. "Take it slowly, there. We don't want you to pass out again." A man ran a cool cloth over her forehead, and the comfort of his touch made her sigh. "You got quite a knocking on that noggin of yours, and I'm afraid you're going to have a lump, too."

She reached toward the back of her head, where the thumping originated, and winced as soon as her fingers brushed her scalp.

11

"I told you," he said. "No touching."

Sebastian. The rock star. The bunker. Earthquake!

"Earthquake? We had an earthquake." She didn't quite remember what had happened, but waking up next to that sultry voice wasn't a regular occurrence.

"Seems like it, with the way the earth was rocking and rolling. I've never felt anything like it. While I've been waiting for you to come 'round, I've been thinking of some new lyrics." Although his words were cheerful, his voice sounded a bit strained.

Glad I could inspire a song.

"What are we still doing down here?" The room sped around her, and her body swayed with it. Was it her, or was it really happening?

"Well, I was hoping you could answer that question as soon as you woke up. You see, after you passed out, I heard all this commotion coming from the door, and I can't seem to get it open."

She groaned. How could she have forgotten to secure everything? Besides which, she'd never imagined getting trapped down here with someone unwanted. "Safety feature."

"What did you say?"

"It's an aftermarket safety feature I'm working

on. Automatic locks. If the bunker is inhabited when the lock's engaged, it won't open for a certain amount of time. It's supposed to keep the looters out, you know? Once some type of natural disaster strikes and people figure out a person has supplies, they become a target. This way, they can't get in."

Sebastian grew quiet, as if pondering the meaning behind what she said.

"How long?" he finally asked.

"What?"

"How long before we're allowed to get out of this blasted hole in the ground?" he snapped.

She took a dry gulp. "Three days."

"No bloody way!"

He sagged against her on the cot and covered his face with his palms. His body shook, as if he were shivering from cold.

"Hey, are you all right?" She reached out to touch his arm.

He drew away. "I'm not going to be able to make it three days. No way in hell. Buried alive."

In the dim light, Kayla noticed sweat pearled on his forehead. It wasn't hot, so she knew it had to be something else. Nerves? Some people were deathly afraid of being trapped underground. Could he be one?

He was inhaling in short bursts. When someone hyperventilated, you gave them a paper bag to breath into, right? Damn. She needed to prepare for first aid, too. She hadn't imagined caring for someone else, especially a rock star with cracked armor.

She stood, much more slowly this time. She needed to take inventory of their situation. She'd always stocked the bunker with food and water for more than one person. Often, she imagined being down here with a friend or family member, or, at a long shot, her sister. The first order of business, aside from tidying herself up, was to get the radio working and check on the situation outside. Then she could decide if she was going to try to crack the lock, or remain put for the time being. Either way, it could be a while.

Sebastian moved toward the door, as if he was going to check it again, then stopped. Rocking back and forth, he mumbled, seeming to talk more to himself than to her. "I knew this was a bad idea. I never should have come. I need to follow my instincts if I'm to get out alive." He turned in her direction. "Tell me there's some special alarm, right? Someone will come looking for you?"

She glanced downward and shrugged. "It's not like a house alarm. I didn't set a panic button. Plus, it's Friday, and I didn't have many plans for the weekend. Maybe if I don't show up at work on Monday, someone will come. What about you?"

"Not likely." He waved his hand dismissively, but it shook. "My people are used to me disappearing for a few days. If I need something, I call. Otherwise, they leave me alone. Creative spirit and all."

His words spewed out faster and faster, and he massaged his chest, his eyes growing wider.

"Hey, are you okay?" she asked, worry spiking. "Don't you black out on me. You're too damn big. My luck, you'll land on me, and where will that leave us?"

"You know how many women would love to be under me?" He sounded on edge, pushing the limits in order to hide his own fears. "And more than a few men, too."

Just like a man. One moment of weakness, and now he had to build himself up again. "That's it. Stroke your ego. As long as you don't faint."

"Who? Me? I'd never faint." He swayed, bracing his arm against the wall.

"Yeah, you. A big guy like you."

Seriously, if he passed out, what was she to do?

15

So they'd experienced an earthquake. It happened all the time in Southern California. Although there might be some problems, it didn't merit him freaking out so much.

"Blast it. You're the freaking survival expert who didn't tie down her supplies. One little earthquake comes along, and what happens? You get knocked off your feet."

She blinked, anger filling her. Here she was trying to help him, and now he attacked her.

He pushed away from the wall, steadying himself. Returning to the chair he'd been sitting in, he picked up his guitar, letting his fingers caress the surface. Humming, he picked out a melody, one that seemed strangely appropriate for the moment, and he seemed to calm.

"What's your name again?" he asked.

With an exasperated sigh, she said, "Kayla," and threw an arm over her eyes, blocking him out. If she couldn't see him, he didn't exist, right? So maybe the locking mechanism on the door wasn't the best solution to the situation. At the time, it had sounded good in her head. Now, trapped with *him*, well.... It could be worse, right?

"Do you have a cell phone?" she asked. Since she

hadn't expected the meetup to last long, she hadn't even bothered to carry hers.

"A mobile phone? Jeez, why didn't I think of that? No service, and the battery's dead."

"I've got solar batteries. We might be able to charge it enough to send a text message. In an emergency, a text message has an eight hundred to one better chance of going through than a call."

Hope soared in Kayla. They might get out of there faster than expected.

"Got a universal charger, too?"

"No." Nothing like having her optimism squashed.

"What makes you do all this?" Twisting from side to side, he surveyed the setup of the bunker. "I don't understand it."

"Don't judge me. If I want to be prepared, how does it harm you?"

He was one of those who'd never understand no matter how many times she explained it. But if you looked at humanity at any point in time, something catastrophic and disastrous always happened. When the chaos went down, she wanted to be ready. Her friends scoffed at her basement hideaway, stocked with water, canned goods, and nonperishable supplies. She also stored blankets and cots and batteries, seeds in packages to keep them dry, solar chargers.

A hidden periscope connected the underground bunker to the outside world so she could check out what was happening if disaster struck. She'd even set up a closet with a composting toilet with tablets to dissolve matter.

Sebastian sat down on the cot with a heavy thud and placed his chin in his hands. "Look at me. I'm stuck down here, with the likes of you. You're one of those crazy prepper nuts, aren't you? I've caught some of those shows on TV."

She couldn't stand people who ridiculed without understanding. So she prepared for natural disasters. So what? People who didn't died every day.

Her chest tightened, and she exploded. "You want to know why? I've lived my entire life in Southern California, listening to the predictions of the 'Big One' when chunks of the state are going to fall into the ocean."

"Or break off and become its own island, right?" he continued for her, his expression skeptical.

"Exactly." She narrowed her gaze, not sure if he was being serious or mocking her. "We've been warned about the San Andreas Fault, which could result in the Big One, but there's many others like the Puente Hills Fault, which runs through Orange County to Downtown Los Angeles. Then, in other parts of the US, we had hurricanes like Katrina and Sandy. 9/11 struck New York and D.C. What do we have here in the West? The Santa Ana winds? The way I see it, it's a matter of time. Why not be prepared?"

"So all of that inspired this?" He swept his arms around the bunker.

"No, my dad's a big influence, too. After being in Vietnam, he wanted to be prepared. He always said he'd seen the best, and the worst, of humanity."

"And your mum?"

"My mom either agreed with Pop or humored him," she said. "But she also grew up in the Midwest, where tornado shelters were common. Not too far of a leap."

"What I don't understand is the entire 'underground' aspect of this bunker." He shuddered. "If this is earthquake country, isn't it safer to be somewhere above ground than buried beneath it? I mean, what if there's some sort of cave-in? How will someone find you? Or us, for that matter?"

Her face flushed hot. Did he not get it? Judging her with his arms folded over his chest. Over the years, she'd run into many who didn't understand. It was one of the main reasons she didn't talk about the issue often. "The idea wasn't to get trapped down here in the middle of an earthquake." Her heart beat faster. She never won these arguments. The other person always went away the victor, feeling self-satisfied, and Kayla was left with her crazy supplies. She shouldn't expect it to be any different this time, when she'd trapped a celebrity in her underground bunker.

"The best thing to do is stay put or to go out into the open somewhere," she continued, feeling her conviction harden. They were in this situation whether they liked it or not. "I've got some reinforced support in the house, places away from the windows that would be a more secure spot to ride out a shaker."

Crossing her arms over her chest, she breathed deep. "It's the time after a natural disaster that can get the trickiest. If something major hit, then would be time to find a secure spot to lay low. We've got all sorts of turmoil happening in the United States. Terrorism. Look at the Boston bombings at the marathon. All made from a household appliance and a child's toy. What about the nuclear meltdown in Japan? Milk from cows in Oregon has tested positive for higher concentrations of radiation." The idea alone was overwhelming. One couldn't hide from radiation poisoning. She could buy pills to counter the effects, but growing crops?

"Yeah, so?" he said.

She ignored the derision in his tone. "We don't know if we're going to see any effects from that," she said. "Don't get me started on the potential collapse of the banking system."

"Is that what you think about? Every day? All the bad things that can potentially go wrong?" Sebastian asked. "Doesn't it make you a bit anxious? I do my best not to think about things like that. A person could drive themselves crazy."

"You want out of here? Fine, go for it." Kayla pointed toward the doorway. "Be my guest and try to break the lock. If you succeed, I make no promises to your safety out there. We don't know what's happening. Maybe this was a minor shaker, or maybe the real thing, but what's it going to hurt to sit tight and figure it out?"

"You plan on helping me pass the time in a more

enjoyable manner?" He wagged his eyebrows at her, and despite herself, and her promise to have a strong will, a flutter started low in her belly. She couldn't be attracted to him. He was such a neophyte. People like him never understood her.

"You watch yourself there." She turned around and stalked to the other side of the room. Okay, given they were in such a small space, there wasn't any getting away from him at the moment. He—and people like him—made her so mad.

"What about being optimistic?" he asked. "Thinking about the best in people. Self-fulfilling prophecies and life affirmations?"

"You can be positive all you want, and it's not going to fill up your tank of gas. Having money, in smaller bills, hidden in case the banks crash and your ATM card doesn't work—that's being prepared. Just because I believe in reserving some supplies doesn't mean I willed all this to happen. It did, and I'm ready for it."

"'Reserving?' Is that what they're calling it nowadays? I thought it was more akin to hoarding."

Hoarding? He really didn't get it. His comment hung in the air, and she did her best to ignore it. No matter what she said, the scorn from nonbelievers hurt. She grew up with her father being harassed by family members. It was only a matter of time before it was her turn. And her sister? Well, forget about telling her anything about being prepared. Maybe as destruction hit and a certain segment of the population was taken out, they'd be all gone. All that would be left would be those who'd taken the necessary precautions.

A wave of dizziness at the implications hit her, and she sat back down.

Right. As if life worked like that.

Chapter Three

S he was gorgeous when she got mad. Even in the low light of the bunker, a red flush shone on her cheekbones, and he'd bet anything her chest was just as flushed. Sebastian adjusted his cock in his pants. Damn, if he didn't have to get trapped with Ms. Superior High-and-Mighty who looked like *Playboy's* Ms. August.

She hadn't said anything about this situation being "God's will" yet, but if the Lord himself had planned on Sebastian getting stranded with a stunning blonde without any soccer games to keep himself entertained, he must have had something up his invisible sleeve.

A sliver of doubt crept into his mind. What if she was correct, that the earthquake had been serious and they were trapped down here for an extended period of time? Panic flared, but he tempered it.

He checked out his guitar leaning against the wall. At least he'd have his tunes to keep him company. He kept saying he wanted to start working on the next album. Why not use this time and do it? In fact, he'd been in a bit of a dry spell. Now, some chords and the refrain, a trill of notes sliding into bass tones, kept rolling through his head.

For as long as he could remember, music had soothed him. When things hadn't gone so well at home, he could kick it in the garden and strum his beauty, drowning out the sounds of his parents fighting inside. As a teen, he'd spent most nights in pubs playing and when he didn't come home at all, no one asked him any questions. He doubted they'd even noticed with all the rest of the kids, the non-troublemakers. Well, his little sister did. Years ago, when Lizzie had nightmares, Sebastian had soothed her the best and he'd always made sure there was food available in the house and her clothes were laid out for the next day before he headed out.

"So what do you think? Does it feel like we're floating in the ocean?" he said to distract himself.

Kayla turned toward him, a slow smile starting as his meaning dawned on her. "Shut up."

His stomach chose that moment to chime in with

an obnoxious growl. It started low in his belly, a churning he knew was coming but couldn't control, and then it broke free, making her burst out laughing.

Grinning, she asked, "Is somebody hungry?"

Sebastian covered it with his hands, as if that would make a difference. "Who knows how long I've been down here with you? I'm starving. And being at your pad so early, I barely had breakfast."

"Early? You were way past lunch," she said.

"Not if my bedtime is often past three in the morning. 'Rock star,' you forget."

All this back and forth was great, helping to keep him distracted, and it had morphed into something more comfortable already. They were together on this adventure for however long, and they might as well make the most of it.

"Oh, how could I? Being in your presence is awe inspiring." She swung her legs over the side of the cot, giving him a flash of curvy calf and a hint of her inner thigh.

His cock hardened. Now? Love among the ruins? In a bunker? He did his best to ignore where they were. The fact the ceiling could cave in at any moment and trap them beneath the earth. Watching the sexiness of Kayla made it all that much easier.

He shifted his stance to make himself more comfortable, and he swore he caught her watching him. When he met her gaze, her eyes widened, and she looked away.

"Here, hold my hand and keep me steady while I get up," he said, just to see what she would do.

She raised her eyebrow and held out her hand, fingers turned down and palm facing her body, as if he was going to kiss it.

He closed his hand over hers and was startled by the silky softness of her skin against his calloused fingertips. As she went to stand, he pulled, and they tumbled backward. She ended up in his arms, all soft plushness with her breasts pushing against his chest, cleavage that made him want to drop his head and forage for nipplage. He settled his free hand on her rounded hip and his fingers splayed out over the curve toward her ass. She licked her lips, causing her bottom one to shine in the dim light like a beacon calling him.

Despite his earlier intentions, his cock pushed out, letting both of them know his interest. Maybe he should apologize. Let her go. Beg off. Instead all honorable and gentlemanesque statements fled from his mind.

Nope. There was one thing he could do—claim her mouth.

In slow motion, he watched her nostrils flare. Time stretched out, and he moved closer.

"Not a good idea," she said, pushing back. She wanted him to kiss her, and she'd almost let him do it, too, but they were in an emergency situation here. It wasn't date night. They weren't at a bar. She never let her hormones get the best of her, and she prided herself on her mental prowess. Sure, it seemed she was a bit of a party pooper, but at least she stayed safe that way.

The Prepper Party Pooper. Fabulous. Just the moniker she wanted to be known by.

"What's up, love?"

She looked over at Sebastian. A grin played over his face, making her shiver, and that annoyed her.

"I don't quite appreciate being called 'love,' and while all this is flattering," she waved her hand in the air between them, "I don't think we're quite a good match. Don't get me wrong. You're hotter than hell, but we're from two different worlds here, and we've got no future."

While the differences between them made him

28

kind of adorable, they also scared her. She could get attached fast. Once they got out of this bunker, she expected him to escape. Better to leave it platonic. Plus, his glib attitude bugged her a bit.

He pulled back. "Are you rejecting me?"

"Rejection? Oh no." She shook her head. *As if he could ever believe someone wouldn't want him.* "If you knew what my body was doing right now, you'd know I wasn't rejecting you."

"So you're hot for me right now?" He advanced. "You want me?"

Gulp. "Umm, how would you define 'want'?"

"Well...." He ran his fingers through the back of her hair, pulling her so close his breath hummed off her cheek. "You've got goose bumps, and I know if I dip my fingers between your legs, I'm going to like the wetness I find."

"I'm not your type," she countered. "Plus, we barely know each other."

"I'd say we know each other well enough. How do you know what my type is? About right now, you're feeling very much my type."

"I'm not in the market for a fling. You travel often. You have...groupies. You'll break my heart and leave me here thinking about you."

"I can promise you, though, it'd be worth it." He ran the tips of his fingers along her cheek, sending shivers throughout her body.

She pulled back, fighting the urge to step into his arms. "Oh, I'm sure you can be pretty good. But this girl is going to continue to resist your charms. Consider me immune."

"I get it. Hands off." He turned both palms toward her.

She flashed him a dirty look. As if she believed him. Guys like him didn't take "no" quite so easily, and part of her didn't want him to stop.

He leaned back, watching her, the perfect image of controlled, suppressed energy, like a cat stalking its prey. "You've got some fancy setup here. Explain the layout to me, so I can get my bearings."

And just like that, he is going to let it go? Whatever. She turned her thoughts to the best way to describe the bunker without being able to turn on all the overhead lights and give a tour.

"Have you ever seen one of those diagrams of a layout of the house? The small boxes to indicate bedrooms, kitchen, living room, and such?"

"Like a schematic?" He seemed interested.

"Exactly. So picture one large room. We're not

quite under the house. More off to the side and cutting under the garage. In the main area, we have shelving around the outside walls and space for our cots. The door is to our right. Opposite us on the north wall is the kitchen area. I've got some cookware set up and food supplies. To the right of that is a bathroom. Nothing fancy, but it offers some privacy."

"So it's like a studio apartment. One bedroom, but optimized for the space."

"Right. Now, some bunkers can get insane. I've seen drawings for separate bedrooms and one even had a sunken tub. Some people buy premade, like a giant round tube. They dig a hole where they want to place it and bury it. Mine's more of a remodeled basement."

"Brilliant." He looked about. "I did a bit of feeling around while you were out, but it's good to know the makeup."

She couldn't help but smile. Was he accepting her? "Before I get some food, I'm going to check out the lock." She grabbed a portable lantern and hung it on a hook near the door so she could have her hands free.

"Shouldn't there be some sort of safety release on it?" As he followed her, his shadow cast over her work area.

"Can you move? I can't see," she said. Even without him touching her, she felt his nearness like the electric currents from his body jumped the space between them and sizzled. If she shifted backward half a step, her body would be flush against his. Rocked by indecision, she lashed out. She could move away, or move closer.

"Sorry, I'm trying to help," he said, stepping back, hands up in surrender.

"You're distracting." Frustration built. She couldn't concentrate on what needed to be done with him...*there*. "Yes, there should be a backup. Always have a back-up plan. A Plan B and a Plan C. Guess what? Those plans don't always work."

With a pencil tip, she attempted to press in the reset hole. A snap and give told her she'd broken the tip off. Why hadn't she thought to store a few paper clips? Paper clips could be used as lock picks in a pinch. Another thing to add to the list.

She banged her fists against the door, rewarded with a deep thud. "I give up. We're not getting out yet." She glared at him, mentally daring him to say something—anything—sarcastic.

He, wisely, said nothing. Her muscles protested

as she stood and stretched out her back, twisting side to side.

"Right," she said, more to herself, wiping off her hands. "So now to check out the radio." At least she'd invested in a good one, with rechargeable batteries, a solar panel, a crank, and an external antenna. She also grabbed an old watch from the same shelf. Almost seven-thirty.

She'd been unconscious for that long? She touched the sore spot on her head, wincing. It could have been so much worse.

The radio powered on with a crackle, and she searched through the stations, static, and voices melding together, until she recognized the familiar voices of the hosts on KFI AM 640.

"Power's out across the Southland. Minor injuries reported." A burst of disruption broke through, cutting out the voices. "105 Freeway closed, checking for structural damage." She could all too well imagine the stretch of freeway closed down for inspection. She hated the long overpass connecting the 405 to the 105. It stretched high up in the air and ended at a stoplight to join the flow of traffic. The last time she'd been on it, she'd gotten caught at the highest point for almost ten minutes. The entire time she was up there, she'd thought, *What if there was an earthquake right now?* She and the rest of the drivers would go plummeting down, cars and all. Maybe not. Engineers in Southern California studied ways to keep everything intact in such situations. Still, did they know what would happen before it struck?

Out of the corner of her eye, she saw Sebastian slump his shoulders. "Not much help at the moment," she said as she turned the radio off. It would be useless to try to look out the periscope at night, when the lights were out. The lack of news was much better than a high death count and looting. She relaxed a bit, but he seemed even more wound up.

"Sounds like we're going to be here for the duration," he said. He cracked his knuckles, picked up his guitar, and settled down on the cot. The music possessed a longing that allured, attracted, and seeped into Kayla's soul.

Chapter Four

They settled into a quiet truce on opposite sides of the bunker. Sebastian stretched out on a cot while Kayla worked in the kitchen, making bread. Working with her hands was relaxing, and gave her freedom to think. The repetition soothed her, plus, there was the added benefit of coming up with something delicious.

From a shelf, she took out a plastic bowl and wooden spoon and added some seven-grain flour, a pinch of brown sugar, baking soda, salt, oil, and buttermilk powder mixed with water. As a secret ingredient, she tossed in dried bacon. She mixed it together then stretched to flick on the fan.

A loud whirling sound erupted in the enclosed space.

"What the bloody hell is that?" Sebastian said, bolting into a sitting position.

Stifling a laugh, she pointed upward. "Exhaust fan. Takes out all the smoke while I cook."

He humphed in response, but got up and watched what she was doing.

She turned on a small portable burner and placed the dough in a pan, covering it and checking her watch. Within a few minutes, the sultry scent of bread seeped out, and she resisted the urge to take a peek.

"What are you making?" He poked around in the food-storage area. "You sure do have a variety down here."

Passing over the first question, she answered, "I tend to get bored eating the same thing over and over." She shrugged. "Sure, basic shelter food may be some nonperishables, but I figure why be boring? If it's the end of the world and we're isolated, then why not bring some delicacies, too."

"No beans 'n franks? I thought canned food would be a staple."

"Don't worry; I've got plenty of that, but I'm also all about whole grains that can be milled. Some complex flours. Might even have a secret stash of chocolate. You know, all those necessities."

"Mmmm, chocolate. Maybe we can melt some on

your hot body later." He gripped her hips, and let his presence be known. His actions earned him a swat away.

"Don't make me burn this. Even with a fan, I don't think burned bread is going to smell good down here."

She grabbed the spatula and slid her hand into a pot holder, lifted the lid, and flipped over the bread, satisfied with the nice browning on one side. Now, to slice salami and a little bit of cheese. As a final thought, she opened a can of olives with a pull-tab and poured them in a bowl. She hated those pull-tabs on a daily basis, but they sure came in handy in an emergency.

After unfolding a small table, she spread out her favorite tablecloth, a cornflower-blue-and-yellow Provence pattern. The cheerfulness infused her with a springtime happiness like a picnic on a sunny, secluded beach, and about now she needed it. Okay, it was really an oversize napkin not a real tablecloth—there wasn't *that* much room down here—but it still had the same effect.

Sebastian had made his way back on the cot and was strumming his guitar again. It seemed like his go-to position. In the few hours they'd been trapped together, she'd learned so much about him, his quirks and idiosyncrasies. So far, she found them both infuriating and cute.

"Are you ready to eat?" she asked, setting out two glasses.

"You can count on it." He approached her with a smile and when his gaze landed on the feast, they grew wider. "Damn. You weren't kidding."

He tucked into the meal and his enthusiasm made the half-hour of cooking worth her time. Nothing like a satisfied customer. The bread had come out crunchy and dense, not as perfect as if she'd baked it in an oven or even a bread machine, but she couldn't beat the quick time and results. Without preservatives, they'd have to eat it within a day or so. By tomorrow morning, it would be hard but still edible.

The perfect bite was composed of a thin slice of bread, topped with salami, cheese, and then an olive on top. She tossed the combination in her mouth and moaned in delight. Maybe next meal, she'd unpack some of the sundried tomatoes, too.

"I like that," Sebastian said, disturbing her culinary fantasy.

When she opened her eyes, he was staring at her.

38

"Like what? The food?"

"The noises you make. I imagine that's what you'll sound like when I make you come. For someone so quiet, you enjoy a lot of the pleasures, don't you?"

She was glad he couldn't see the full blush on her cheeks in the dim lighting. She looked down, coming back to center. He'd delved deep into her psyche, too. Since she spent so much time alone, she made sure not to scrimp on the finer items. Who knew when the Big One, the big earthquake would come along? She could prepare as much as possible, carry an emergency kit in her car, keep a stockpile at home. Still, the future was uncertain. Having someone to share it with, right now, changed her perspective a bit.

Instead of it being her against the world, they were in the disaster situation together.

A flush of emotion made her self-aware. When Kayla had put together this hideaway, she'd thought of just about everything. Too bad she hadn't packed any condoms.

When she didn't answer his question, Sebastian dropped it. "If your family is all prepared for a natural disaster, where are your parents?" he asked.

"Will they be worried?"

Glad he had left it alone, she said, "A few years ago, they moved to Missouri. The earthquake in Japan, tsunami, and nuclear meltdown, made my dad want to be in a more centralized part of the US. On the Pacific Coast, we're too close to potential fallout. Have you seen some of the tracking of waste that's made the journey across to our shores?"

He nodded. "Sure. I've heard blokes say some have taken years."

"That we know of. Those are the larger pieces. Probably more we don't know about."

"We shouldn't fear what we can't see," he said, tapping the table with the bottom of his glass.

"Or maybe we should fear it even more."

Stalemate. They grew quiet and continued to eat.

Sebastian took a long drink of water. She watched his Adam's apple move as he swallowed.

"Only you and your parents, then? No siblings," he said.

"I've got a sister, too," she said. "She's a few years younger than me and lives in San Diego."

Mackenzie was in grad school, and Kayla hoped she was all right. For living so close, they didn't talk much, but she didn't hold any hard feelings against her.

Sebastian raised an eyebrow, waiting for her to finish.

"She's not a believer," she said.

"Doesn't have a bunker in her home?" he asked, looking around.

"Nope. You know how some people come from a strict religious family, and they grow up with opposing views, kind of like a backlash? That's Mackenzie. Drives her car down to fumes, keeps enough food in the house to last a week at most. The last time I opened her fridge, I found a few yogurts and Diet Coke. Oh, and a box of leftover pizza, and her cupboards are even worse."

"She thinks you're nutters?" he said.

His accent combined with the word "nutters" made his comment even funnier. She hadn't heard the term before, but it perfectly described how her sister saw her—to the extreme. She laughed, feeling the mood brighten. "Probably as much as I think she's irresponsible. What about you?"

"I've got one older brother and two younger sisters," he said. "We don't all get together often. The youngest, Lizzie, still lives at home."

"Do you miss them?" she asked.

"Only Lizzie."

She got up and brought the plates over to the sink.

"Can I help you at all?" he asked, moving close enough so she could once again feel his presence.

"Not now; we'll see how long this goes on for."

He rinsed off his hands before returning to his music. His fingers slipped into the starting position, and he strummed.

Chapter Five

C lose quarters. Despite the amenities of the premises, Sebastian couldn't ignore they were underground forever. Every time his mind fluttered to that, his heart stuttered and his palms grew damp. Putting aside the guitar, he tracked Kayla's movements. She moved with efficiency, cleaning up after dinner and taking stock of the supplies. He needed a distraction, and Kayla proved to be the best one around.

"You going to keep avoiding me all night?" he said.

With a half-turn, she glanced at him. "I'm not. I'm just tidying up. You can entertain yourself."

He wasn't so sure. Left alone, he tended to get into trouble. In this type of situation, it was even worse.

"I thought that was your job," he lobbed back to

her. He wanted a reaction, a fight, a smile, something.

"I'm no longer on the clock. We're in survival mode now."

She squatted down, real low, searching for something on the bottom shelf of a rack. She pushed until satisfied with whatever she was doing.

Although petite, she was a fireball of energy. He was more used to women who liked to be pampered, not ones who took care of him without some sort of ulterior motive. Sure, her agency wanted his account, but he knew there was something between them. It wasn't like he shagged every available woman.

Why was he pushing the issue of attraction? He wasn't hard up or anything. Outside the bunker, he had plenty of women throwing themselves at him, but then Kayla was intense, serious, and he liked the contrast. Despite whatever came with it, the video shoot had introduced him to her. If they could not get rescued, then maybe he'd make the best of it.

Once finished, she stood with her hands on her hips and studied their surroundings. Time to make his move. He drew closer, testing the waters between them. Would she continue to flee from his advances?

She glanced at him and a slight flush lit up her

cheekbones. The only sign of emotion. He wanted to rile her up, get a real reaction. As an artist, he displayed his emotions through his songwriting. He wanted to know the real her.

"Why don't I take out my notebook, and we can write some of those fears down? You know, voicing your fears can sometimes help get rid of them."

"I'm not afraid." Despite her strong words, her voice trembled.

The smoothness of her cheek called out to him, and he ran his fingertips down the side, his thumb grazing over her lower lip. She seemed more comfortable flying solo. He glanced around the bunker. Despite having ample supplies, she hadn't counted on being holed up with someone she didn't know.

"What are you hiding from, down in here? Life?"

She brushed aside his comment with a flick of her hand, turning away from him. "You don't know me, and you don't get to judge me." Her voice quivered.

"Excuse me for trying to care," he said. This time, rather than deflecting, he pursued, placing his hands on her shoulders and turning her around. "I want to know you better."

He stared down at her mouth. "Fuck it." He kissed her and her soft lips opened under his. A whisper of feeling, lips brushing against lips. Her breath tickled his mouth, and he pressed in harder, wanting more and taking more.

She opened, granting him access to her tender tongue. He ventured forth, stroking his tongue over her full bottom lip before deepening the kiss. Hesitantly at first, the tip of hers touched his, and then the slow, sensuous dance began.

She melted into his arms, plush against his hardness. She tasted sweet, like the chocolate she'd mentioned earlier. Had she snuck a piece during dishes? He grew light-headed, and his passions warred. He knew better than to get involved with her, but he still wanted her—badly. How could one unassuming woman turn his life so upside down, and so quickly? Or maybe, she was making it right-side up.

Sebastian ground his hips against her, his cock instinctively seeking entrance of another kind. Each stroke of his tongue brought their bodies closer together. He moved his hands around Kayla's waist, over her lower back, to rest on the top of her ass. He reined himself in from going further. He didn't want to scare her away by moving too fast. Oh, how he wanted to cup her arse and lift her against him. As if she knew exactly what he was thinking, she moaned against his mouth.

Sebastian's libido spiked, and he was more turned on than he had been in a very, very long time.

He kissed her with all the creative energy and pent-up passion he'd been holding back. Kayla nibbled on his lower lip, and he maneuvered them around to push her against the wall. He held onto her hands, bringing them up above her head, as if holding her chained in place. What would it be like to have his way with her body to do as how he'd like? Her mouth opened farther and he plundered. His body took the cues from his mind, and his spirits lifted. She may be the one able to heal him.

And all this from a kiss.

When they broke away, she breathed heavily and an adorable flush brightened her cheeks. A bit of pride flared in his chest.

"Wow, what was that all about?" she asked.

"I've been wanting to do that for hours, and it was better than I had hoped." He smacked his lips. "Hey, were you sneaking chocolate on me?"

"Whoops," she said, covering her mouth. "You

47

caught me. I promise I was going to share."

"Right. Naughty girl."

She worried the corner of her nail, retreating into herself. He didn't want to push too hard, too fast, so he let her go. He leaned in, barely touching his lips against hers. "Brilliant."

"What?"

"You're brilliant. You make me feel alive."

Kayla's eyes widened, and she nodded. "It's only nine-thirty; what do you want to do?" She rushed over to a cabinet and opened it. Inside were a heap of board games.

Oh, he could think of a whole bunch of things instead of the board games occupying her attention. A kiss like that deserved to be followed up with further ravishment. The earth rumbled, giving them a quick jolt. His pulse rate skyrocketed.

"Aftershock," she said, holding onto the shelf.

Just as fast, it stopped. "That one wasn't so bad." He did a mental countdown to calm his nerves and found himself not as panicked.

"Just a temblor." Holding a game of Scrabble out, she asked, "White flag?"

"Wow, haven't seen one of those in forever. I'm used to playing the electronic version on my mobile."

He cracked his fingers in an exaggerated stretch. "But I'm sure I can manage old school."

They laid the board on the cot between them, and each picked a single tile from the bag to decide who went first.

"So, are we playing dirty Scrabble?" he asked, selecting his seven tiles.

"Does everything go back to sex with you?"

"It's my masking mechanism," he said. If she only knew the truth. "Hard to think about dire circumstances when your sensual synapses are on overload. How about rather than keeping score, we trade points for kisses?"

She ignored the explanation. She tended to close up when she didn't know what to say.

"Color," he said, laying out his word. "C-o-l-o-u-r."

"Hey, hey, US spelling please. No U."

"What? Says who? You didn't lay out those rules."

"We're in America. By default, we go by our spelling."

With a grumble, he picked up the U and scooted in the r. "There, happy now?"

"Very. L-o-c-a-l."

"No need to rub it in. I've got my working papers."

"Do you live here full-time then?" she asked, leaning over the game board.

"Mostly, when I'm not on tour. The studios we're working with are in States, so I am, too."

The heaviness of their earlier conversation dissipated. After he played his next word, he caught her staring out into space, looking past him. What could she be thinking about? Maybe their kiss. It affected him more than he let on. What made her so different than the other women he'd been around? For one thing, she didn't giggle or gush all over him. She treated him as if he was...normal.

He watched her. "Hey, earth to Kayla. Your turn."

"What?" She blinked and focused on him.

Pointing to the board, he said, "L-o-s-e. 'Cause that's what you're going to do."

"Keep talking big. B-a-c-k."

"Why yes, I would like a back massage."

***

After an hour, the space on the board grew tight

and she stifled a yawn.

"Why don't we finish this game in the morning?" he said. "It's not like it or we will be going anywhere." Carefully, he lifted the board and moved it onto the table. "Usually, I'd be up much later than this, but I'm beat. Maybe it's the lack of stimulus." He could have kicked himself. "Wait, I didn't mean that like it sounded."

"No worries. I understand. It's kind of like being up in a mountain cabin. Sure, the altitude has an effect, but it's also the mental relaxation. Something tells me in your real life you don't get a whole lot of downtime."

"Not much. When I'm on the road with the band, I've learned to sleep almost like they say they do in the military—wherever and whenever. It's not the getting to sleep bit I tend to have a problem with, it's the staying asleep part."

She looked at him with her head tilted to the side, probably trying to figure him out. He wasn't going to offer any further explanation. Hopefully, he wouldn't wake her with any of his antics tonight.

"I like to get my eight hours," she said. "I'm going to go wash up. I'll put an extra toothbrush out for you."

"Extra toothbrush," he muttered as she walked away. She thought of everything. But she wasn't prepared for the likes of him. He didn't want to scrub away the taste of her. Right now, all he wanted was more.

Chapter Six

Something had woken her, and she wasn't sure what. She lay still, holding her breath and listening to the darkness. Earlier in the night, she'd enjoyed Sebastian's company more than she'd expected. When he wasn't acting all macho, he was quite kind. Her stomach did a little flip-flop as she remembered the feel of his lips. She was attracted to him. What living, breathing woman on this Earth wouldn't be? After being alone with him for the day, she'd already seen past the pretty-boy exterior to the complexity and wit beneath. How often did he let his guard down?

Even though he was a celebrity, Kayla figured he had a public and a private side. Look at her. She was certainly different at work than at home or around friends and family. Maybe she should give him, and herself a break, and do what she could to enjoy the next few days. Take this little trapped-in-the-bunker excursion like being stranded on a deserted island, have a fling. Who was the last guy she'd dated? Jimmy from Sales? Boy could that man talk without taking a breath.

A whimper disturbed the even sounds of Sebastian's slumber. She moved closer to his cot. His brow furrowed, and his eyelids twitched. Was he having a nightmare?

"Shhh," she soothed. "It's all right. You're safe."

Without any idea what he was dreaming about, all she could think to do was offer comfort. Earlier, he'd seemed panicked about being trapped in the bunker. Growing up in earthquake country, she was pretty jaded when it came to the shakers. For someone new, it could be extremely frightening. Maybe those fears were coming through his dreams, twisting reality into horror. She stroked his hair, wanting only to soothe, not disturb.

The lines across his forehead smoothed out, and the tightness of his body relaxed. Once his breathing became more even, she went to stand. His reached his strong arms out, wrapping them around her body, and pulling her against him.

"Stay," he murmured, nuzzling against her neck.

His body felt so warm and safe, she obliged, telling herself only for a few moments until he feel deeper asleep.

***

Kayla woke to a hardness pressed into her backside. As the drowsiness lifted, she realized what she was feeling. What would it be like to wake every morning like this, in a man's arms, safe, secure, and wanted? But that wasn't reality. She shouldn't fool herself into having the dream. She attempted to wiggle into a different position.

"Keep doing that, and he's really going to wake up," Sebastian said. "Excuse the morning wood. He doesn't know any better."

He stuck his hand between their bodies, copping a feel of her ass as he shifted his cock to the side. "Thanks for keeping me company last night."

"It seems like you were having some nightmares. Do you remember anything?"

"Not much." He shifted his gaze away, and she guessed he remembered more than he wanted to tell.

Kayla got out of bed and decided to clean herself up.

"Where are you going?" he mumbled.

"Time to start the day."

"Already? Slave driver." He turned over, flinging his arm over his head.

Shaking her head at his antics, she pulled the curtain on the washroom area. She filled the basin with a small amount of fresh bottled water. She'd thought about having regular plumbing run down here, but at the same time she didn't want to have to rely upon the system.

Dipping a washcloth in the basin, she massaged her chest and neck, cringing as she reached the soft spot on the back of her head. Stupid to not secure the canister. It should have been one of the first things done for safety in earthquake country. Sure, the shelves themselves were tied up, and the walls reinforced, but she needed to do some more work on the bulkier items on the shelves.

After a rinse out of the washcloth, she turned her attention to the lower half of her body, enjoying the sensation of the cloth between her legs. From the feel of him hard against her, she imagined Sebastian gave some good loving.

If it was the end of regular civilization, he just might be a good candidate for a mate. She blushed at the thought. Resourceful, strong, and sexy as hell. And then there was his voice. When she awoke to the sound of his singing after being knocked out, it was like she had been transported to another sensual world. Check that. Maybe he wasn't a good candidate; she'd have to fight off too many other women.

After finishing up, she rinsed out the cloth, hung it to dry, and then yanked the plug on the basin. For now, it ran off into an oversize bucket, which would only last for so long. In another area of the shelter, she had a built-in drainage pipe that flowed discretely down a hill behind her house.

From a set of drawers, she removed a tank top, a fluffy sweater, a pair of underwear, and sweatpants. She hadn't packed away any sexy survival wear, just the basics of comfort and need. Maybe she'd have to fix that for the future.

She took a mental inventory of the supplies they had, and what needed to be done over the next few days.

Although the bunker had been stocked, she wasn't prepared for what being isolated underground for an extended amount of time entailed. While she had the physical location and it was well stocked, it was different in practice. They were locked in, without an escape route, but when they got out, she'd have to take into consideration being secluded for a longer period.

***

After breakfast, Sebastian strummed his guitar, and what came out of it sounded more and more like a complete song.

Always, though, Kayla was aware of his physical presence. The more time passed, the more he consumed the space. If she ran, he'd follow. If she shied away, he might pounce. His thigh brushed hers under the table, and her entire body heated up. When their hands touched while washing dinner dishes, she thought of him caressing her naked body. Lewd mental snapshots consumed her thoughts with every turn, every touch. Her desire strung taut, almost to the breaking point.

Instead of continuing to fight it, maybe she should give in to her longings.

The evening drew on, and they finished the game of Scrabble, with Kayla winning—narrowly.

"What would you like as your prize?" he asked as they sat on the cot.

Heat rose in her cheeks. "A kiss."

She leaned in, closing the gap between them. He pushed the game board to the floor, the tiles tumbling everywhere. For a brief moment, his breath blew hot against her mouth, and then lips touched lips, and she pushed aside the self-doubts to experience this moment. This kiss was nothing like the first.

This one Kayla knew was coming, but still it surprised her. The magic they'd shared before flared right away, proving without a doubt the attraction wasn't a fluke.

Sebastian nibbled her bottom lip, and heat flushed through her. She opened—her mouth, her heart, and her body—to him.

He slid his hands around her back, bringing her to him as he laid her on the cot. His hard cock pressed into her abdomen. The physical connection between them had nothing to do with being in an emergency situation, and everything to do with chemistry. They wouldn't be dying anytime soon. He sizzled with sexiness, and she found herself unable to resist.

As he continued to kiss her, he pulled off her sweater. Underneath, her nipples stretched the material of her tank top. She didn't remember ever being so turned on, anticipating what came next. Forget what her mind kept arguing against; even if it was for this moment, she wanted Sebastian.

"Hello, sunshine," he said. "Look how gorgeous these breasts are."

Off went the next layer, and her breasts fell forward, asking for attention. Right away, he took a nipple in his mouth and sucked, flipping his tongue against the tip and making her arch into him. As he sucked, he made wet noises, which turned her on even more. He supported her back with his other hand, holding her in place.

In his arms, under his attention, she felt beautiful and confident.

"That feels so fucking good," she said.

His mouth stilled. "Kayla! Your language."

She ditched her conventions. No one else was there to judge her and what she wanted to do. In the outside world, she had to act a certain way. Here, trapped with Sebastian, a whole different set of rules existed—or didn't. He gave her permission to be free.

"Fuck my language. Right now I don't want to be prim and proper, or worry about if I'm ruining or securing our chances of landing your account. I just want you."

"You have no idea how good that makes me feel," he said. "Too many of the women I meet are concerned about the rock star, not the person I am."

"Rock star? Do I know you? Are you someone famous?" she teased him.

"Funny one," he said, and then tweaked her nipple with his thumb and middle finger.

A moan escaped her. God, did he ever know how to excite her.

"Stand up for me," he said. She obeyed, letting him slide her pants all the way down to the floor.

A chill hit her bareness, but disappeared when he replaced the material with his hands. She shivered beneath his touch. He slipped two fingers between her legs, pressing against her silky underwear. "Mmm, so very wet. Is all this for me?"

She shifted, hoping to encourage him to travel farther.

"Uh-uh, patience."

Swirling, twirling, he moved his fingers around in a figure eight, ratcheting up a higher emotional response.

He brushed his lips against her stomach, flicking his tongue into her belly button. Her body quivered.

His hair prickled the underside of her breasts.

"That tickles." She lounged on the cot, resting on her elbows, an open invitation. "Come join me?"

"I thought you would never ask."

He settled next to her, leaning her back farther. He smelled woodsy. Half his body covered hers, one knee pressed between her legs, spreading them farther apart. His weight reassured her, steady and secure, and then he brushed down her panties, exposing her pussy to his touch. His middle finger found entry first, sliding inside her and tilting up below her clit.

Her body shuddered. Damn. Why hadn't she done this more often? Too much isolation, and not enough interaction. The feeling of being touched, consumed, settled through her while at the same time put her on edge. She wanted more, and now. His long hair fell over his forehead, and his eyes were half-closed. Deep in concentration, he rubbed her with his thumb, and she moved with him.

"Does that feel good, baby?"

"Mmmm, yes. Don't stop." His magic fingers caressed, drawing her out of her shell stroke by stroke. He built up her lust, and her heart conquered her fears. Her desire cranked up, as if he were winding an engine, even tighter.

"Don't plan on stopping for a long time. How long did you say we had down here?"

"Three days—" Her breathing hitched as he sank another finger inside her and leaned over, flicking his tongue over her clit. He covered her with his warm mouth, circling and massaging.

"And we already wasted one. I suppose that'll be enough time to thoroughly work you over." He gave her a wicked smile and then mouthed her pussy, not stopping until she'd draped her ankles over his shoulders and cried out his name.

"You, I want you," she said, digging her nails into his shoulders. He pulled off his T-shirt and she traced the outline of the tattoo on his rib cage. She'd caught a glimpse of ink on his side earlier when he'd stretched, but hadn't been able to make out the design, a circle with a blue bar intersecting it.

She trailed her fingers over the letters. *Underground*. His skin prickled beneath her touch.

"Is this for your band?"

"Pretty much," he said, taking her hands and bringing them up to his lips. He sucked on her fingertips, sending shivers down her arms.

She unbuttoned his jeans, and he lifted his hips

as she slid the pants down. When she reached his briefs, he stilled her hands.

"He may look a bit different than you're used to?"

What in the world is he talking about? "Huh?"

"My cock. He's uncut."

Her mind tried to translate what he was saying: Uncut? She hoped his cock wasn't cut. Who would cut a man's...? "Oh, uncircumcised."

"That's right. So he may have more parts than you're used to."

"Well, thanks for the warning. I would have figured that out."

"It's just been my experience in America, you know. Some women get a bit turned off."

Was this big, macho singer apologizing for the way his cock looked?

As she gripped him through the material, he rewarded her with a deep moan. "Does it work the same as a circumcised one?"

"Oh, yeah."

"Then that's all I need to know."

With a quick shove, she chucked his underwear and wished to hell the lighting was better. Then again, by the feel of him alone, he was huge—thick and long. Maybe she wouldn't want a closer look after all.

"Show me how to touch you," she said, caressing him. The thought alone turned her on. He held onto his cock and stroked up and down. The covering undulated. "It adds another layer of friction," he explained between gritted teeth. "At least that's what I think."

Placing her hand over his, she caught the rhythm. She couldn't close her fingers around him. The foreskin was soft, and a bit of pre-cum seeped out of the end. She slid her thumb over it, mimicking the way he'd done it earlier.

"If we're going to continue this liaison, you're going to have to stop. That feels too good."

She hesitated, fighting with desire. "I want you, but I don't have anything here. No protection."

Sebastian didn't want to throw her, but he was packing.

"No worries there. I always carry some," he said.

Next to him, she stilled. The lovely motion stalled, and he wondered if he'd said the wrong thing. Maybe he shouldn't have admitted to being prepared?

"You have condoms?" She leaned backward, and his poor cock stuck straight up, abandoned and sad.

"Sure. In my guitar case. Inside pocket." He'd had that little feature installed to hold special items. Guitar picks and a few rubbers always came in handy.

"I'm not sure I want to ask right now, but go get 'em," she said.

He was back in the game. When he set off on this adventure, he never would have guessed he'd find a woman like her or get trapped in a bunker with her before taking a tumble. He would have figured it would be some boring exploration, not worth his time. By feel, Sebastian found the pocket on the inner lid of the guitar case. A slight tug on the clasp opened it and he slipped out a foil packet, making a quick count of the supply. Plenty to keep them busy.

"You get lost over there?"

The more turned on she got, the more sultry her voice sounded. Right now, she could do phone-sex calls. He wanted to make her cry out his name again, but this time buried deep inside of her.

Always the quiet ones.

"I'm coming," Sebastian said.

"Not yet, but you will be soon."

"Promise?"

He ripped open the wrapper and slipped on the protection. With how wet she was, he wished they could go at it bareback, but safety first and all that.

He stumbled, and a metal clang rang out before the pain hit his foot. "Bugger." He'd fucking kicked something fucking hard. "Bloody buggering storage can."

"Are you all right?"

"I will be." He fumbled forward a few more steps, hands outstretched, feeling his way until warm flesh came under his fingertips. "Oh, that's more like it."

Creamy thighs, not too muscular, not too soft. Right between her legs he moved, thrusting upward, kneeling until his cock hit her entrance, slick and ready for him. He slid in a few inches before coming back out.

"Are you sure you want to do this?" he asked, partially for her but also for him. If she stopped him, he might escape unscathed. Something told him he wouldn't be able to forget this woman easily.

"Absolutely." She lifted her hips. "Let's make the Earth move."

As he pushed into her pussy, her words echoed in his mind, a new mantra. Each pump, he repeated to the refrain. She stretched upward, finding his mouth, and the unison of their tongues synched up with their bodies. Her warmth embraced him, caressed every inch of his cock, and soothed his fears. Pure lust consumed all hesitations. He gripped under her ass, pounding into her. She met him thrust for thrust. His entire body heated up, and he slowed the pace, stringing out every sensation. She smiled and ground her hips upward, adding a different friction to the mix.

Two could play that game. He rubbed her clit with his thumb. "Do you like getting fucked?" he said, egging them both on. "Come for me. Show me how good it feels."

Her inner walls tightened around him as her orgasm overtook her. She sucked on his upper arm, adding a bit of pain to the pleasure.

He wasn't ready to come yet. He wanted more of her. He pulled out, eliciting a whimper.

"Can you roll over for me?" he asked, guiding her body over and her ass up in the air.

Two plush globes of her rounded arse greeted him. Sweat from their romp shone on her skin, leaving it glistening. He licked the hollow of her lower back as he fit himself between her legs and delved in.

"Yes, stretch me." She moaned, rocking back on

his cock.

He pumped into her, his balls bouncing off her mons, until she grunted with each plunge. The pleasure tightened the base of his cock, and his body stiffened as he came. He swore it went on forever, her moans matching his own.

Wiped out, physically and emotionally, he lay on his side, pulling her over with him. Their breathing leveled out, and the gentle rise and fall of her chest moved under his hand.

He kissed her shoulder and whispered, "My muse."

***

She slept within his arms while he thought about his music. For so long, it had fueled his passion. Being on stage, strumming his guitar, creating. All the background noise—the marketing and kissing up to those who didn't give a fuck—like ad-sales representatives, thanks a lot—wasn't his thing. But when it came to his music, he took an active role. If a video was going to be shot, it had to live up to his standards, and that was why he'd made the trip. Not because he possessed high expectations for a payoff, but because he wouldn't settle for anything less than perfection.

Right now, a new form of perfection snuggled against him. He'd avoided attachments for so long, thinking they might be a distraction from his career. But maybe, that didn't have to be the case. He could have both. Maybe, he needed both.

A song floated through his head, something he hadn't heard in so long.

He stared down at her in his arms, marveling. Twenty-four hours trapped with this woman and one rambunctious shag, and his writer's block had dissipated.

Chapter Seven

Panic struck the moment Sebastian woke. Heart racing, he sat up to darkness. He fumbled beside him, searching for a lamp but found only open air. Where the hell was he? The events of the previous day crashed upon him, he remembered the earthquake, the shelter...and Kayla.

Where was she?

He couldn't breathe. Like someone sat on his chest or held the covers over his head for too long. His thoughts drifted back to that day, so many years ago, and he fought to regain control of his emotions.

He reached down next to the cot, found the portable lantern this time, and flicked on the switch. There she was, sleeping in the cot next to his but still too far away. The shallow light cast a shadow over her face, long eyelashes standing out against her pale skin and her lips parted. For someone so intense during the waking hours, she appeared peaceful while she slept.

Why had she moved from sleeping next to him? Maybe he had gone a little crazy. He tended to kick the covers off and talk in his sleep, especially when the nightmares hit, a tidbit the guys in the band liked to tease him about on long bus tours where no one had any privacy.

Or could she have moved for another reason altogether? Regret over getting physical with him?

He'd have to ask after she woke. It had to be morning by now. He couldn't believe how much he wished for natural lighting, to stare up at the sun and feel its warmth against his body. It was one of the main reasons he now resided almost full-time in Southern California. He loved England, but the dreary days of his homeland got to him. Sunshine, more days of the year than not, was more his style, and he was thankful his career afforded him the option to choose.

Not to mention he had to escape. Too many bad memories.

The day before had had its highs and lows. Discovering Kayla hurt and not being sure what to do, had rocked him to his core. He didn't have to take care of such things; he had people for those types of duties but yesterday, he'd had to take control and figure out the situation. When he'd done so, a sense of pride and independence had fueled him.

Being buried deep inside her hours earlier.... It might not have been the smartest thing he'd ever done, but his body enjoyed it and, if he admitted it, so did his mind.

It was different being with someone so normal. She wasn't a groupie, or a fellow rock star. Her life was uncomplicated, and he'd come along and screwed with it. When they got back to the real world, she was going to hate him because of the noise his life brought. For now, he'd take what he could get, and maybe she'd help chase the nightmares away.

The terrors persisted. He couldn't get free of them, no matter what he tried to think about. His throat constricted. Suffocating. Thick black smoke filled the small compartment. The already blacked-out confines grew even darker. When the train—the tube—lost power, everything turned off, even the emergency lighting. Fire from somewhere added smoke and his nostrils burned while he tasted ashes on his tongue. He wiped soot from his eyes, only to have them clog right back up.

And then the moans and screams began, cries for help over the creaking metal. He coughed, breathing tainted air. Light from mobile phones shattered the darkness. He fumbled in his back pocket for his, praying for service. The brightness burned his eyes for a moment, and he wiped away the dust again, feeling it smear across his forehead. A baby bawled and his heart ached.

They were trapped, and he had no idea how long it would be before help arrived.

"Shhh, it's all right. You're safe," a voice like an angel called out to him. He fought the cloying web of the nightmare, seeking the light. He hovered in the between world, semi-asleep, and semi-awake, where nightmares felt the most real.

"Please wake up." The voice again, soothing.

He lurched upward, gasping, and she was there, taking him within her arms, enveloping him in her warmth. Bloody nightmares. He must have fallen back to sleep.

She brushed back his hair.

"What was it? Maybe if you talk about it, it would be better? It might help you let it go."

"I don't talk about it." His voice sounded raspy, like it had that day. "Stupid dreams won't leave me alone. When can we get out of here?"

Her body tensed against him. Guilt filled him. Bloody hell, all she was trying to do was help him and instead he pushed her away, when he really wanted to hold her close.

"I didn't mean to pry. Just trying to help. We're stuck here for a while." She handed him a bottle of water. "Here. Sounds like you might need this."

Although it was room temperature, the liquid soothed his raw throat. Had he been screaming in his sleep? What a mess. He must have scared the hell out of her.

"Listen, I'm sorry. I have these recurring nightmares, and I hate the feeling of being trapped."

"Claustrophobia. I get it." She watched him. He avoided her gaze. "Lots of people have it. Being stuck in a bunker doesn't help it much either. Let me tell you a secret—I live in Southern California, the land of freeways, and I hate overpasses. Every time I'm at the top of one, I imagine an earthquake hitting and sending me and all the other drivers plummeting."

"Didn't that happen before? I remember something." Even though he'd been living in L.A., on and off, he rarely considered the potential of quakes.

"Yep. Northridge quake, 1994. I was a kid then.

It was bad, but the San Francisco area has had some worse ones."

"Well, see, that's a learned phobia," he said.

"Don't change the subject. Are you telling me yours is not learned? Oh, I forget. Mr. Rock Star doesn't share personal information with me."

She returned to the cot, and the absence of her body, her physical presence, left him with a void. He wanted her back, but knew he'd have to give something in return. Himself.

"I stayed the night out at a mate's place, but I promised my little sister I'd be home for her birthday. I wouldn't normally be on such an early tube—too many office workers—but I didn't want to disappoint Lizzie." When he started talking, his voice took on a haunting quality to his own ears, as if someone else was telling the story of that day.

Not much else would make him get up so damn early. "I was dozing, with my head propped up against the glass, and my guitar tucked under my arm, when the explosion hit. It took me a while, but I realized...we'd been bombed."

"It was all over the news," she whispered. "You lived through that? Good Lord, when was that?"

"2005. The London Underground bombings,

they called it." The horror of it rolled over him again. "Fifty-two people dead, seven hundred injured. I came out whole in body, but it changed my life." As he said the words, he realized how true they actually were.

She stilled, completely focused on his tale, and all he could hear was the beating of his own heart.

"The tube jumped the tracks, and the whole carriage turned on its side. There were murmurs of all sorts about what could have happened. It had been a while since the IRA hit."

She moved back to his bed, bringing a lantern. The warm glow chased away the shadows. It was as if they were encircled in a magic sphere of safety, and the world outside of it remained unknown.

She took his hand and climbed under the blanket with him. "How long were you in there?"

Memory flashed—blood in the darkness, and how it appeared black. Reaching to help someone and coming away with wet hands. Wiping them on his jeans. He'd fought against panic and the need to escape. He had to help others. A woman's arm, barely connected to her body. Trying to stop the bleeding with another guy's belt. He couldn't tell her all of that. The horror remained too fresh in his mind. At night, when it was quiet, he heard the echo of their screams, and he hated the dark. His fear lingered too close to the surface. Sometimes he felt like if he gave it a holding, it could take over his life.

He swallowed and took another sip of water. "Time is weird in an event like that. An hour, maybe a bit more, but it feels much longer, and I know it could have been worse. Once my body figured out it was all together and whole, that flight nature kicked in. I had to fight with myself to make sure others were all right, too. Not everyone was."

God, people had died. He'd been bloody lucky to get out intact. So fucking lucky.

"Here I've spent my entire life frightened of what might happen someday, and you lived through it and survived it," She rubbed his arm. "No wonder you don't like being underground."

He needed to finish the story and purge the memories. "Mobile phone service worked for shit in the tunnels, but I used the light. I'd forgotten to charge it overnight, so it didn't last long. When I got out, when I saw the sun again, even though it was clouded over, it was like my soul had been shaken out and sparkled anew. I don't remember too much more about what I saw. I know it was horrific, but a mind is

78

a powerful thing. Blocked some memories."

And he edited the content for her sensibilities. He hunched over, the telling of it exhausting him.

"Your family must have been so relieved when you got home."

He shrugged. "I didn't get home until much later that day. Dirty, torn, and bloody clothing, still carrying my damn guitar. I must have looked like the walking dead. I remember dropping it when Lizzie launched herself into my arms. Never thought I'd smell her sweet baby hair again, or feel her small hands against my face. When I didn't come home, they'd known I might have been on the Underground, but not if I was alive."

She watched him, searching his face, as if she wanted to ask him something but was afraid. Afraid to make him angry or afraid of his answer?

Finally, she asked, "You never got any help for it? Or talked to anybody?"

"Why? Because I have nightmares?" Sebastian became defensive. People who'd never lived through such a thing really couldn't understand. "People lost limbs and loved ones. Me? I got off light. Can't stand confined spaces, though. And trains. Let's say I'm glad I'm in Los Angeles, the land of roads and cars."

Dryness scratched at his throat, and he sipped water. She'd grown quiet and still, not asking any further questions, and he could almost feel her thinking, putting the pieces together.

"The band's name, the UK Underground, it ties into that day, doesn't it? And your tattoo."

He'd been waiting for her to make the connection. "Yes. Before then, we hadn't settled on a name. Afterward, it seemed quite appropriate."

"But how come I've never heard the story? The band is connected more with the underground music scene."

He chuckled. "People will interpret what they want. Why would they connect me, the band, and the Underground bombings I don't want to capitalize on other people's pain."

He and his bandmates had discussed the issue from time to time. One of the most often asked questions in interviews was how the band got its name but he always deflected. Those few hours had scarred him, brought him to the realization he couldn't take life for granted. At any moment, everything he held dear could be blown away.

A light kiss brushed against his neck. Soft lips, warm breath. "You are a complicated and amazing man." Her voice dropped to an almost whisper. "Remember, it's your pain, too."

An argument bubbled up inside of him, and then just as quickly disappeared. She was right. He'd been running away from the trauma so much he'd forgotten his own pain. The experience was one he couldn't control, and he'd never know if something else would ever occur. He possessed no influence. Natural disasters, terror attacks, happened everywhere. He needed to do more than live. He needed to embrace life.

Music remained his rock, his center. He never doubted the guitar in his hands, or his ability to entertain others. What he doubted was his ability to connect with them. To give himself emotionally to another person.

For fear of losing them?

The truth struck him, nearly as fast as they had been trapped in this damned underground bunker. How could he be stuck and free at the same time?

"Anyone ever said you should go into psychology?" he asked, giving her a tight hug. "You're a miracle worker."

"Don't give me credit." Kayla smiled, returning his hug. "Some people overcome their fears by facing them. For someone with extreme claustrophobia, trapping you down here was like throwing you into the deep end of the pool in order to teach you how to swim. I just got lucky to be the one here with you."

No. He was the lucky one.

Chapter Eight

Time lagged the next day. Sebastian watched Kayla bustle about the small space. She warmed with her tasks, she wore fewer and fewer clothes, and she'd pulled her thick hair up off her neck. Tendrils escaped, and one stuck to the side of her cheek. He wanted to reach out and smooth the hair off her face. Didn't she feel the blasted thing? It was driving him crazy.

Within tight quarters, they kept getting in each other's way. He couldn't jump her every time she brushed by him, and his cock rose to attention.

Although his lower anatomy had a different idea about the situation and despite being under lockup, he enjoyed the time spent with her. The warring of the words, and the kissing.

She blew out a small breath, and the section flounced upward, then boomeranged back. Stuck again. A rustling of plastic broke the silence as she opened individual packages of cookies and arranged them on a dish. She popped one into her mouth. "Why are you staring at me like that?" she finally asked.

Telling her it was because she looked adorable while aggravated wasn't going to get him anywhere. Despite her preparations, she seemed to be going as stir-crazy as him. Right now, she fought with the plastic of the cookies a bit too much.

"I like watching you." He shrugged. What was wrong with that? I wasn't like they had any other form of entertainment.

"Want some Biscoffs?" Kayla asked.

"What are they? Biscuits?"

She held them up. "Oh, speculaas, I see," he said. "Toss me a couple."

"They travel and store well," she explained. The small white packages with the red writing shot through the air like tiny, sweet missiles.

He bit into the hard cookie, savoring the way it burst into flavor against his tongue.

"Thanks."

The sound of her shuffling a deck of cards broke the quiet. Her hands folded the cards inward, mixing them with ease. She tapped-tapped-tapped them against the table and shuffled again. Even in this act, she liked things precise. Could she live in the chaos of his world?

"Strip poker?" he asked, knowing the answer but still hopeful.

"You wish."

"Well, I did get you to strip last night, and we weren't even playing games. What's the incentive this time?"

Her smile flashed big. "Who gets to be on top?"

"You've got yourself a game." He twirled the seat around to sit on it facing the back and leaned his elbows against the table.

"Let's make it a little fairer to start with." After undoing a few buttons, he rolled his shoulder out of his shirt and batted his eyelashes at her.

"Oh, come on!" She flicked a few cards at him.

"Hey, you're pretty good at that."

"Plenty of practice."

"Uh-oh, don't tell me you're a cardshark."

"Then I'll make sure not to tell you." She shook her head at him and dealt the hand. "Five-card draw."

He watched Kayla's expression as she picked up her cards: blank. Hmmm, she held a good poker face.

85

He did his best to set his and then picked up his own hand. Three aces to start. Was it a setup? The serious way she studied at her own cards and moving them around as if they were magically going to transform into something else told him she wouldn't stack his deck.

"I'll take two, please." He pushed them across the table toward her.

"And dealer takes one," she said.

Damn. One card. What could she be holding? Please, please let me get a good hand.

Two kings. Hells, yes! A full house. Aces over kings. Almost impossible to beat those odds.

"I call," she said.

Slowly, he laid down each card, and her eyes grew wider. After his last one, he reached over and tapped the bottom of her jaw shut.

"Now show me what you got."

"You won. No worries there." She put the deck back together then.

"No fair. You called, and I showed. What do you have?"

With a sigh, she laid down three jacks and two tens—another full house. "Ooooh, so close," he commiserated.

"Sure, I can see you're all torn up about it. Better to take your contacts off before we go there. You wouldn't want them to wash out from all that crying."

She stuck out her tongue. He grabbed the tip and gave it a little squeeze, eliciting a screech from her.

"You better watch out, or I'm going to make you use that thing," he warned.

"I'd like to see you try." She reshuffled the cards. "Double or nothing?"

"No freakin' way. You didn't say best out of three when we started. Now that I'm ahead, I want to take advantage of the situation. I want to take advantage of you. Let me tell you a little game me and the band picked up here in the good ol' U S of A—fifty-two card pickup." He grabbed for the deck, split it in half, and aimed upward.

"No, don't do that!"

They shot upward and rained down upon them. Kayla laughed until tears ran down her face.

"Now weren't you saying someone got to choose being on top?" Sebastian took her hands in his. "I think I want you on top and utilizing that tongue of yours. It seems to need a bit of exercise."

As they moved across the bunker, toward the cots, he kissed her. Like an accelerant to a flame, passion flared out of control. He'd have her again right here, right now. They should be looking for an escape, or hatching some sort of a plan to conquer the locked door, but the moment their lips met, though, all thoughts of escape fled. She tasted like the cookies, all cinnamon sugar, sweet with an underlying spicy flair. After such a short time together, he was discovering her many layers and her complexity intrigued him.

He pushed down her shorts, happy to find bare arse under his wandering hands.

"What's fair is fair." She returned the favor by removing his borrowed sweatpants. A burst of cool air brushed over his cock. Like she didn't want to know when he'd stocked the condoms in the guitar, he didn't want to know about the change of men's clothing in the shelter.

"Who got the top, winner or loser?" she asked.

"You," he said, lifting his hips upward. "The answer would be you."

"Good." She stroked him, exposing the tip of his cock, and then leaned forward to envelope him in her mouth. She cupped his balls, massaging gently, as she sucked.

Eyes closed, he took in the sensations. Every

88

nerve in his body fired sensual alerts. If this was how they'd pass the time together, he'd be happy to stay. The warmth of her mouth disappeared and he opened his eyes. She leaned over and grabbed a condom from their stash and put it on him.

"Ready for me?" She straddled him.

The moment of anticipation stretched, and his heart ached for the moment to last forever. She looked at him with longing and desire, her eyes half-mast and her mouth turned up in a sultry smile.

He didn't bother to answer. His cock jumped at the question.

She sank onto him, sighing as she took him to the hilt. Bracing her, he held onto her hips, thrusting upward as much as possible. She rode him hard, head tossed back and her clit rubbing against his pelvic bone. Their movement shook the cot beneath them, while overhead, the shelves shuddered.

Couldn't be, could it?

"Aftershock," she said, clamping down hard and increasing the rhythm. "Let's ride it out."

Her moans of pleasure came out in a staccato of pants as she came. Once stilled, she draped her lush body over his and trembled. He ran his fingers along her damp back and thrust upward, taking his fill. His orgasm lasted longer than the temblor.

With a contented sigh, she slipped off and cuddled beside him. Her breathing settled as she drifted off to sleep.

Still wired, his mind turned toward the lyrics floating about his head, his writer's block gone

Bunker Girl

You bring sunshine to the darkness.

Light to the shadows

And love to my life.

***

He couldn't sleep. It was the third night, and maybe their last.

Sebastian's heart raced as he lay in the dark, thinking about her and his life up to this point. He hadn't opened himself up to the possibility of a relationship. Sure, he dated, and he'd been with more than his fair share of women, especially the first few years on the road, but that had grown old quick. They'd all been a gaggle of giggles with bouncing boobs and no depth. They all wanted to touch the magic, steal a piece of him, but, after the sex, a hollowness had filled him, as if they removed a chunk of his soul when they'd left his bed.

He ran a hand through his hair. All in all, it sounded a bit melodramatic, and he definitely wasn't a drama queen. He supposed he'd gotten something in return. Some sort of muse, energy sucker that he was. Time passed; it had worn him down. When the screaming crowd chased after him, he ran. Let the bodyguards earn their money.

He pushed aside the callous thought.

This past year, he'd spent more time isolated, working on his next album, or so the publicity wranglers explained. In truth, he was hiding from the darkness threatening to smother him, licking his wounds, and praying for the musical muses to return. He couldn't find them in mindless parties or alcohol-induced slumbers. A tropical-island vacation proved to be a waste of time. All he came home with was a peeling back from a rubbish sunburn. Who decided it was a good idea to shove the Brit in the hot sun with some oil?

In order to stay relevant, they needed something new, the reason his manager had insisted upon shooting this new video. It would be kind of a quirky documentary promo. Instead, he'd found his inspiration dug deep beneath the earth.

Kayla threw her arm over her head and mumbled in her sleep. Energy consumed the woman during her waking hours. Rather than be at peace while asleep tonight, she didn't rest. Maybe dreams plagued her. Or maybe she was the one who needed an island vacation.

Images of pouring oil over his palms, warming it, and then spreading it over her bikini-clad body filtered through his mind. With the canary-yellow dress she'd been wearing the first day, he could imagine her in a bathing suit of the same hue. Whenever he saw the color from now on, he'd forever think of her and this time spent together.

How could he ever forget?

So what was it about this one? She knew who he was, and she didn't care. She'd seemed uncomfortable when they first met, even put off. His celebrity didn't impress her, and while she looked downright cute in her sunny dress, she hadn't dressed super sexy and provocative, like many other women in the same position would.

Nope, she hadn't been focused on selling herself. Instead, she'd wanted to get him in and out in as short an amount of time as possible.

Maybe he should be thanking Mother Nature for

causing the earth to quiver, trapping them together. Turned out to be quite beneficial after all. Plus, the shadows in his mind had receded. The impossible had happened. He'd been trapped underground again and survived. Brushing back a lock of her hair, he embraced Kayla as she settled her body against his. He watched the steady rise and fall of her bare breasts, relishing the feel of where she pressed against him. She tucked her head under his chin, and rested one hand on his.

What did her actions mean? Did he have the same calming effect on her. For some reason, the thought gave him solace. He wasn't the only one invested in this thing between them—what kind of relationship could they possibly have after they'd been trapped in the bunker together for two days? The closeness they shared wasn't only in his imagination.

Something within him also called to her. She trusted him, too. Trusted him with her body, and her soul. Would she move aside some of the blocks in her heart and let him have a place there, too?

He might have some work cut out for him, but if the past few days had taught him anything, it was he had some pretty damn good survival instincts himself.

If he wanted a spot in Kayla's heart, he'd have to prove himself to her. He wasn't quite sure how. She'd not only built up this physical bunker to keep herself protected, but she also had more than a few walls of safety around her heart, too.

Time and persistence were keys, and maybe some good loving.

Chapter Nine

Chewing on the end of a pencil, Sebastian seemed deep in thought. Kayla watched as he pulled the pencil from his sinful lips, made a note, and then closed the notebook.

She caught a flash of silver. "What's that?"

"Songwriting book." He held it up.

"No, I saw something. Do you have a paper clip?"

"Yep. A lazy-guy bookmark."

She kneeled next to him, and held out her hand. "Let me have it."

"My marker? What for?"

"A lock pick." His eyes grew wide and he smiled, handing it over.

She unfolded the metal, careful not to snap it. Paper clips might be worth pennies, but this one was priceless.

With the key to their exit in the palm of her

hand, she hesitated. Sebastian wagged his eyebrows at her. Once they got out of there, though, who knew what would happen? Despite how close they'd grown, outside lay the real world, and their lives didn't mesh. Would their time together be over?

But the fear of what life would be like on the outside wasn't a reason to stay trapped in the bunker. She unfolded the metal and put the paper clip into the lock and jiggled. If she hit the internal mechanism just right, it would pop open. The clicking of the opening locks resounded with a finality that tugged at Kayla's heart. Their time together was over.

"You did it!" Sebastian picked her up and twirled her around, as much as he could in such a confined space.

Putting on a brave face, she said, "Ready to go out there?"

"Hell yes!"

She understood his enthusiasm. Really, she did. But did he have to be so excited to get out of the bunker, away from her?

She'd kept him entertained, mentally and physically, and now he was ready to leave her—and the time they'd spent together—behind. It wasn't like they could stay in there forever. She hesitated, thinking she should have waited the last few hours before the door opened by itself. They'd spent so much talking about themselves, and yet they hadn't discussed what would happen once they got out.

The metal cooled her hands, and a chill crept into her bones. She closed her eyes, telling herself to be strong. Whatever happened, would happen. She couldn't change the outcome, and a few more hours wouldn't make a difference.

"Here, help me push the door open," she said.

Side by side, they leaned their shoulders against the heavy door, until something gave on the other side and they came tumbling out. Sunlight blinded her, and she shielded her eyes.

"I never thought I'd ever be so happy to see the sun again," he said, squinting. "Forget about wishing I was a vampire because I love the night so much. Now I understand the hardship of going without sunlight."

He barreled up the walkway. "Come on," he said, looking back and holding out his hand. "What do you want to do first? Microwave some popcorn? How about taking a hot shower with me?" He raised his eyebrows in a comical come-hither expression.

Despite the tumble of emotions plaguing her, her

mood lightened. He made it impossible for her to stay serious, which was one of the things she liked about him.

"Maybe we should call and check in with a few people first," she suggested. "You know, those people who might have been looking for us? I should call my sister and catch the news, see if there was any damage."

"So practical, you are," he replied, stopping again, this time to give her a kiss. "Maybe we can even make love later, in a real bed."

The use of the word "later" caught her attention. "You're not going to rush out of here and leave me behind?" That was her ultimate fear. Not another natural disaster, but him walking out and dropping her like nothing had happened between them. Like he hadn't made love to her and etched himself into her heart.

"Are you crazy? I only just got to meet you, and not under the best of circumstances either. After all we went through, you're going to be hard-pressed to get rid of me."

Her pulse picked up. "You live in the fast lane of a freeway, and I move at the pace of a school zone. What could you gain hanging out with me?"

Now at the back door to her house, he stopped. "Seriously? Are we going to have to go through this now? I understand insecurities, but you're a gorgeous, intelligent, and self-sufficient woman. The only woman I know who has an emergency bunker hidden in her backyard."

"Fine lot of good it did us these past few days. We were lucky not to have been buried alive in that earthquake."

He shuddered, and she wished she could have taken back the "buried alive" statement.

"Don't belittle yourself," he said, standing back and letting her enter first. "We've had enough scrutiny and downers over the past few days. Right now, it's time to celebrate our freedom."

Inside her house, everything looked the same— comfortable, familiar, and inviting. She longed to stretch out on the couch and turn on the television. It dawned on her it wouldn't be the same again. Being stuck with Sebastian had changed her.

Over the past few days, she'd thought about his question about "hiding" from everybody. His observation shook her to the core. She'd always been prepared. It was how she was raised. Recently, others had caught up with the trend, but the thought that isolating herself was akin to running scared. Well, it was a reality she didn't quite want to face.

She turned toward him. She had a question she wanted to ask, but at the same time was afraid of it. Usually, her boss at the agency handled the closing of the deals. This one was all her, and she had more at stake.

"Can you lead me to your shower?" Sebastian asked, oblivious to her distress. "I need to clean up, and I can't wait to feel the hot water. I hope you're not one of those women who like it lukewarm; we're going burning."

She stopped, watching him, as if ready for him to turn into a mystical creature she didn't know if she believed in. Could he be everything she imagined?

"Really, Sebastian, what are your plans?"

At his pause, her stomach tightened. She looked away, noticing a new crack running down one wall.

He moved closed to her, until his breath tickled the back of her neck. "Why did I come here? To rent the bunker for the latest video with my band." He leaned in, kissing behind her ear. "It's perfect, and think about the connection of singing the new song there."

Her hopes soared. Could he be saying what she

thought he was?

"And you do know," he said, slipping his hands around her waist and drawing her close, "I'm going to need someplace to stay while we do the shooting...."

Right now, the real world wasn't looking all that scary. "I might be able to help out with that."

"I was hoping you'd volunteer. You wouldn't mind if I stayed up late and practiced, would you?"

"No worries," she said, a grin loony with happiness hurting her cheeks. "If you get too loud, I've got a bunker you can use."

Storage Tips

Louisa Bacio used to work for a magazine focused on American survival. One specialty feature was on the proper storage of whole grains, using a mill at home, and making breads.

Flour must be stored in a cool, dry place. It is suggested you store the flour in plastic bags, freeze for two days to kill any sort of inherent insect, and then store in a sealed container. Ground flour is expected to last at least seven months. If stored properly, unground hard wheat is estimated to last upward of thirty years.

Ideally, a shelter should be stocked with several types of products: immediate use, long-term use, and seed for planting for the future.

About the Author

A Southern California native, Louisa Bacio can't imagine living far away from the ocean. The multi-published author of erotic romance enjoys writing within all realms – from short stories to full-length novels.

Bacio shares her household with a supportive husband, two daughters growing "too fast," and a multitude pet craziness: two dogs, five fish tanks, an aviary, hamsters, rabbits, hermit crabs and rolly pollies. In her other life, she teaches college classes in English, journalism and popular culture.

You can visit Louisa at:
http://www.louisabacio.com